SECOND SIGHT

SECOND SIGHT

by Alan E. Nourse

(Note: The following excerpts from Amy Ballantine's journal have never actually been written down at any time before. Her account of impressions and events has been kept in organized fashion in her mind for at least nine years (even she is not certain when she started), but it must be understood that certain inaccuracies in transcription could not possibly have been avoided in the excerpting attempted here. *The Editor.*)

*

Tuesday, 16 May. Lambertson got back from Boston about two this afternoon. He was tired; I don't think I've ever seen Lambertson so tired. It was more than just exhaustion, too. Maybe anger? Frustration? I couldn't be sure. It seemed more like *defeat* than anything else, and he went straight from the 'copter to his office without even stopping off at the lab at all.

It's good to have him back, though! Not that I haven't had a nice enough rest. With Lambertson gone, Dakin took over the reins for the week, but Dakin doesn't really count, poor man. It's such a temptation to twist him up and get him all confused that I didn't do any real *work* all week. With Lambertson back I'll have to get down to the grind again, but I'm still glad he's here. I never thought I'd miss him so, for such a short time away.

But I wish he'd gotten a rest, if he ever rests! And I wish I knew why he went to Boston in the first place. Certainly he didn't *want* to go. I wanted to read him and find out, but I don't think I'm supposed to know yet. Lambertson didn't want to talk. He didn't even tell me he was back, even though he knew I'd catch him five miles down the road. (I can do that now, with Lambertson. Distance doesn't seem to make so much difference any more if I just ignore it.)

So all I got was bits and snatches on the surface of his mind. Something about me, and Dr. Custer; and a nasty little man called Aarons or Barrons or something. I've heard of him somewhere, but I can't pin it down right now. I'll have to dig that out later, I guess.

But if he saw Dr. Custer, *why doesn't he tell me about it?*

*

Wednesday, 17 May. It was *Aarons* that he saw in Boston, and now I'm sure that something's going wrong. I know that man. I remember him from a long time ago, back when I was still at Bairdsley, long before I came here to the Study Center. He was the consulting psychiatrist, and I don't think I could ever forget him, even if I tried!

That's why I'm sure something very unpleasant is going on.

Lambertson saw Dr. Custer, too, but the directors sent him to Boston because Aarons wanted to talk to him. I wasn't supposed to know anything about it, but Lambertson came down to dinner last night. He wouldn't even look at me, the skunk. I fixed *him*. I told him I was going to peek, and then I read him in a flash, before he could shift his mind to Boston traffic or something. (He knows I can't stand traffic.)

I only picked up a little, but it was enough. There was something very unpleasant that Aarons had said that I couldn't quite get. They were in his office. Lambertson had said, "I don't think she's ready for it, and I'd never try to talk her into it, at this point. Why can't you people get it through your heads that she's a *child*, and a human being, not some kind of laboratory animal? That's been the trouble all along. Everybody has been so eager to *grab*, and nobody has given her a wretched thing in return."

Aarons was smooth. Very sad and reproachful. I got a clear picture of him—short, balding, mean little eyes in a smug, self-righteous little face. "Michael, after all she's twenty-three years old. She's certainly out of diapers by now."

"But she's only had two years of training aimed at teaching *her* anything."

"Well, there's no reason that *that* should stop, is there? Be reasonable, Michael. We certainly agree that you've done a wonderful job with the girl, and naturally you're sensitive about others working with her. But when you consider that public taxes are footing the bill—"

"I'm sensitive about others exploiting her, that's all. I tell you, I won't push her. And I wouldn't let her come up here, even if she agreed to do it. She shouldn't be tampered with for another year or two at least." Lambertson was angry and bitter. Now, three days later, he was still angry.

"And you're certain that your concern is entirely—professional?" (Whatever Aarons meant, it wasn't nice. Lambertson caught it, and oh, my! Chart slapping down on the table, door slamming, swearing—from mild, patient Lambertson, can you imagine? And then later, no more anger, just disgust and defeat. That was what hit me when he came back yesterday. He couldn't hide it, no matter how he tried.)

Well, no wonder he was tired. I remember Aarons all right. He wasn't so interested in me, back in those days. *Wild one,* he called me. *We haven't the time or the people to handle anything like this in a public institution. We have to handle her the way we'd handle any other defective. She may be a plus-defective instead of a minus-defective, but she's as crippled as if she were deaf and blind.*

Good old Aarons. That was years ago, when I was barely thirteen. Before Dr. Custer got interested and started ophthalmoscoping me and testing me, before I'd ever heard of

Lambertson or the Study Center. For that matter, before anybody had done anything but feed me and treat me like some kind of peculiar animal or something.

Well, I'm glad it was Lambertson that went to Boston and not me, for Aarons' sake. And if Aarons tries to come down here to work with me, he's going to be wasting his time, because I'll lead him all around Robin Hood's Barn and get him so confused he'll wish he'd stayed home. But I can't help but wonder, just the same. *Am* I a cripple like Aarons said? Does being psi-high mean that? *I* don't think so, but what does Lambertson think? Sometimes when I try to read Lambertson I'm the one that gets confused. I wish I could tell what he *really* thinks.

*

Wednesday night. I asked Lambertson tonight what Dr. Custer had said. "He wants to see you next week," he told me. "But Amy, he didn't make any promises. He wasn't even hopeful."

"But his letter! He said the studies showed that there wasn't any anatomical defect."

Lambertson leaned back and lit his pipe, shaking his head at me. He's aged ten years this past week. Everybody thinks so. He's lost weight, and he looks as if he hasn't slept at all. "Custer's afraid that it isn't a question of anatomy, Amy."

"But what is it, then, for heaven's sake?"

"He doesn't know. He says it's not very scientific, but it may just be that what you don't use, you lose."

"Oh, but that's silly." I chewed my lip.

"Granted."

"But he thinks that there's a chance?"

"Of course there's a chance. And you know he'll do everything he can. It's just that neither of us wants you to get your hopes up."

It wasn't much, but it was something. Lambertson looked so beat. I didn't have the heart to ask him what Aarons wanted, even though I know he'd like to get it off his chest. Maybe tomorrow will be better.

I spent the day with Charlie Dakin in the lab, and did a little work for a change. I've been disgustingly lazy, and poor Charlie thinks it's all his fault. Charlie reads like twenty-point type ninety per cent of the time, and I'm afraid he knows it. I can tell just exactly when he stops paying attention to business and starts paying attention to *me*, and then all of a sudden he realizes I'm reading him, and it flusters him for the rest of the day. I wonder why? Does he really think I'm shocked? Or surprised? Or *insulted*? Poor Charlie!

I guess I must be good enough looking. I can read it from almost every fellow that comes near me. I wonder why? I mean, why me and not Marjorie over in the Main Office? She's a sweet girl, but she never gets a second look from the guys. There must be some fine differential point I'm missing somewhere, but I don't think I'll ever understand it.

I'm not going to press Lambertson, but I *hope* he opens up tomorrow. He's got me scared silly by now. He has a lot of authority around here, but other people are paying the bills, and when he's frightened about something, it can't help but frighten me.

*

Thursday, 18 May. We went back to reaction testing in the lab with Lambertson today. That study is almost finished, as much as anything I work on is ever finished, which isn't very much. This test had two goals: to clock my stimulus-response pattern in comparison to normals, and to find out just exactly *when* I pick up any given thought-signal from the person I'm reading. It isn't a matter of developing speed. I'm already so fast to respond that it doesn't mean too much from anybody else's standpoint, and I certainly don't need any training there. But where along the line do I pick up a thought impulse? Do I catch it at its inception? Do I pick up the thought formulation, or just the final crystalized pattern? Lambertson thinks I'm with it right from the start, and that some training in those lines would be worth my time.

Of course, we didn't find out, not even with the ingenious little random-firing device that Dakin designed for the study. With this gadget, neither Lambertson nor I know what impulse the box is going to throw at him. He just throws a switch and it starts coming. He catches it, reacts, I catch it from him and react, and we compare reaction times. This afternoon it had us driving up a hill, and sent a ten-ton truck rolling down on us out of control. I had my flasher on two seconds before Lambertson did, of course, but our reaction times are standardized, so when we corrected for my extra speed, we knew that I must have caught the impulse about 0.07 seconds after he did.

Crude, of course, not nearly fast enough, and we can't reproduce on a stable basis. Lambertson says that's as close as we can get without cortical probes. And that's where I put my foot down. I may have a gold mine in this head of mine, but nobody is going to put burr-holes through my skull in order to tap it. Not for a while yet.

SECOND SIGHT

That's unfair, of course, because it sounds as if Lambertson were trying to force me into something, and he isn't. I've read him about that, and I know he wouldn't allow it. *Let's learn everything else we can learn without it first*, he says. *Later, if you want to go along with it, maybe. But right now you're not competent to decide for yourself.*

He may be right, but why not? Why does he keep acting as if I'm a child? *Am* I, really? With everything (and I mean *everything*) coming into my mind for the past twenty-three years, haven't I learned enough to make decisions for myself? Lambertson says of course everything has been coming in, it's just that I don't know what to do with it all. But somewhere along the line I have to reach a maturation point of some kind.

It scares me, sometimes, because I can't find an answer to it and the answer might be perfectly horrible. I don't know where it may end. What's worse, I don't know what point it has reached *right now*. How much difference is there between my mind and Lambertson's? I'm psi-high, and he isn't—granted. But is there more to it than that? People like Aarons think so. They think it's a difference between *human* function and something else.

And that scares me because it *just isn't true*. I'm as human as anybody else. But somehow it seems that I'm the one who has to prove it. I wonder if I ever will. That's why Dr. Custer has to help me. Everything hangs on that. I'm to go up to Boston next week, for final studies and testing.

If Dr. Custer can do something, what a difference that will make! Maybe then I could get out of this whole frightening mess, put it behind me and forget about it. With just the psi alone, I don't think I ever can.

*

Friday, 19 May. Today Lambertson broke down and told me what it was that Aarons had been proposing. It was worse than I thought it would be. The man had hit on the one thing I'd been afraid of for so long.

"He wants you to work against normals," Lambertson said. "He's swallowed the latency hypothesis whole. He thinks that everybody must have a latent psi potential, and that all that is needed to drag it into the open is a powerful stimulus from someone with full-blown psi powers."

"Well?" I said. "Do you think so?"

"Who knows?" Lambertson slammed his pencil down on the desk angrily. "No, I don't think so, but what does that mean? Not a thing. It certainly doesn't mean I'm right. Nobody knows the answer, not me, nor Aarons, nor anybody. And Aarons wants to use you to find out."

I nodded slowly. "I see. So I'm to be used as a sort of refined electrical stimulator," I said. "Well, I guess you know what you can tell Aarons."

He was silent, and I couldn't read him. Then he looked up. "Amy, I'm not sure we can tell him that."

I stared at him. "You mean you think he could *force* me?"

"He says you're a public charge, that as long as you have to be supported and cared for, they have the right to use your faculties. He's right on the first point. You *are* a public charge. You have to be sheltered and protected. If you wandered so much as a mile outside these walls you'd never survive, and you know it."

I sat stunned. "But Dr. Custer—"

SECOND SIGHT

"Dr. Custer is trying to help. But he hasn't succeeded so far. If he can, then it will be a different story. But I can't stall much longer, Amy. Aarons has a powerful argument. You're psi-high. You're the first full-fledged, wide-open, free-wheeling psi-high that's ever appeared in human history. The *first*. Others in the past have shown potential, maybe, but nothing they could ever learn to control. You've got control, you're fully developed. You're *here*, and you're *the only one there is*."

"So I happened to be unlucky," I snapped. "My genes got mixed up."

"That's not true, and you know it," Lambertson said. "We know your chromosomes better than your face. They're the same as anyone else's. There's no gene difference, none at all. When you're gone, you'll be *gone*, and there's no reason to think that your children will have any more psi potential than Charlie Dakin has."

Something was building up in me then that I couldn't control any longer. "You think I should go along with Aarons," I said dully.

He hesitated. "I'm afraid you're going to have to, sooner or later. Aarons has some latents up in Boston. He's certain that they're latents. He's talked to the directors down here. He's convinced them that you could work with his people, draw them out. You could open the door to a whole new world for human beings."

I lost my temper then. It wasn't just Aarons, or Lambertson, or Dakin, or any of the others. It was *all* of them, dozens of them, compounded year upon year upon year. "Now listen to me for a minute," I said. "Have any of you ever considered what *I* wanted in this thing? *Ever?* Have any of you given that one single thought, just once, one time when you were so sick of thinking great thoughts for humanity that you let another thought leak through? Have you ever thought about what kind of a shuffle I've had since all this started? Well, you'd better think about it. *Right now*."

"Amy, you know I don't want to push you."

"Listen to me, Lambertson. My folks got rid of me fast when they found out about me. Did you know that? They hated me because I *scared* them! It didn't hurt me too much, because I thought I knew *why* they hated me, I could understand it, and I went off to Bairdsley without even crying. They were going to come see me every week, but do you know how often they managed to make it? *Not once* after I was off their hands. And then at Bairdsley Aarons examined me and decided that I was a cripple. He didn't know anything about me then, but he thought psi was a *defect*. And that was as far as it went. I did what Aarons wanted me to do at Bairdsley. Never what *I* wanted, just what *they* wanted, years and years of what *they* wanted. And then you came along, and I came to the Study Center and did what *you* wanted."

It hurt him, and I knew it. I guess that was what I wanted, to hurt him and to hurt everybody. He was shaking his head, staring at me. "Amy, be fair. I've tried, you know how hard I've tried."

"Tried what? To train me? Yes, but why? To give me better use of my psi faculties? Yes, but why? Did you do it for *me*? Is that really why you did it? Or was that just another phoney front, like all the rest of them, in order to use me, to make me a little more valuable to have around?"

13

SECOND SIGHT

He slapped my face so hard it jolted me. I could feel the awful pain and hurt in his mind as he stared at me, and I sensed the stinging in his palm that matched the burning in my cheek. And then something fell away in his mind, and I saw something I had never seen before.

He loved me, that man. Incredible, isn't it? He *loved* me. Me, who couldn't call him anything but Lambertson, who couldn't imagine calling him Michael, to say nothing of Mike—just Lambertson, who did this, or Lambertson who thought that.

But he could never tell me. He had decided that. I was too helpless. I needed him too much. I needed love, but not the kind of love Lambertson wanted to give, so that kind of love had to be hidden, concealed, *suppressed*. I needed the deepest imaginable understanding, but it had to be utterly unselfish understanding, anything else would be taking advantage of me, so a barrier had to be built—a barrier that I should never penetrate and that he should never be tempted to break down.

Lambertson had done that. For me. It was all there, suddenly, so overwhelming it made me gasp from the impact. I wanted to throw my arms around him; instead I sat down in the chair, shaking my head helplessly. I hated myself then. I had hated myself before, but never like this.

"If I could only go somewhere," I said. "Someplace where nobody knew me, where I could just live by myself for a while, and shut the doors, and shut out the thoughts, and *pretend* for a while, just pretend that I'm perfectly normal."

"I wish you could," Lambertson said. "But you can't. You know that. Not unless Custer can really help."

We sat there for a while. Then I said, "Let Aarons come down. Let him bring anybody he wants with him. I'll do what he wants. Until I see Custer."

That hurt, too, but it was different. It hurt both of us together, not separately any more. And somehow it didn't hurt so much that way.

*

Monday, 22 May. Aarons drove down from Boston this morning with a girl named Mary Bolton, and we went to work.

I think I'm beginning to understand how a dog can tell when someone wants to kick him and doesn't quite dare. I could feel the back of my neck prickle when that man walked into the conference room. I was hoping he might have changed since the last time I saw him. He hadn't, but I had. I wasn't afraid of him any more, just awfully tired of him after he'd been here about ten minutes.

But that girl! I wonder what sort of story he'd told her? She couldn't have been more than sixteen, and she was terrorized. At first I thought it was *Aarons* she was afraid of, but that wasn't so. It was *me*.

It took us all morning just to get around that. The poor girl could hardly make herself talk. She was shaking all over when they arrived. We took a walk around the grounds, alone, and I read her bit by bit—a feeler here, a planted suggestion there, just getting her used to the idea and trying to reassure her. After a while she was smiling. She thought the lagoon was lovely, and by the time we got back to the main building she was laughing, talking about herself, beginning to relax.

15

SECOND SIGHT

Then I gave her a full blast, quickly, only a moment or two. *Don't be afraid—I hate him, yes, but I won't hurt you for anything. Let me come in, don't fight me. We've got to work as a team.*

It shook her. She turned white and almost passed out for a moment. Then she nodded, slowly. "I see," she said. "It feels as if it's way inside, *deep* inside."

"That's right. It won't hurt. I promise."

She nodded again. "Let's go back, now. I think I'm ready to try."

We went to work.

I was as blind as she was, at first. There was nothing there, at first, not even a flicker of brightness. Then, probing deeper, something responded, only a hint, a suggestion of something powerful, deep and hidden—but where? What was her strength? Where was she weak? I couldn't tell.

We started on dice, crude, of course, but as good a tool as any. Dice are no good for measuring anything, but that was why I was there. I was the measuring instrument. The dice were only reactors. Sensitive enough, two balsam cubes, tossed from a box with only gravity to work against. I showed her first, picked up her mind as the dice popped out, led her through it. *Take one at a time, the red one first. Work on it, see? Now we try both. Once more—watch it! All right, now.*

She sat frozen in the chair. She was trying; the sweat stood out on her forehead. Aarons sat tense, smoking, his fingers twitching as he watched the red and green cubes bounce on the white backdrop. Lambertson watched too, but his eyes were on the girl, not on the cubes.

It was hard work. Bit by bit she began to grab; whatever I had felt in her mind seemed to leap up. I probed her, amplifying it, trying to draw it out. It was like wading through knee-deep mud—sticky, sluggish, resisting. I could feel her excitement growing, and bit by bit I released my grip, easing her out, baiting her.

"All right," I said. "That's enough."

She turned to me, wide-eyed. "I—I did it."

Aarons was on his feet, breathing heavily. "It worked?"

"It worked. Not very well, but it's there. All she needs is time, and help, and patience."

"But it worked! Lambertson! Do you know what that means? It means I was right! It means others can have it, just like she has it!" He rubbed his hands together. "We can arrange a full-time lab for it, and work on three or four latents simultaneously. It's a wide-open door, Michael! Can't you see what it means?"

Lambertson nodded, and gave me a long look. "Yes, I think I do."

"I'll start arrangements tomorrow."

"Not tomorrow. You'll have to wait until next week."

"Why?"

"Because Amy would prefer to wait, that's why."

Aarons looked at him, and then at me, peevishly. Finally he shrugged. "If you insist."

"We'll talk about it next week," I said. I was so tired I could hardly look up at him. I stood up, and smiled at my girl. Poor kid, I thought. So excited and eager about it now. And not one idea in the world of what she was walking into.

Certainly Aarons would never be able to tell her.

*

SECOND SIGHT

Later, when they were gone, Lambertson and I walked down toward the lagoon. It was a lovely cool evening; the ducks were down at the water's edge. Every year there was a mother duck herding a line of ducklings down the shore and into the water. They never seemed to go where she wanted them to, and she would fuss and chatter, waddling back time and again to prod the reluctant ones out into the pool.

We stood by the water's edge in silence for a long time. Then Lambertson kissed me. It was the first time he had ever done that.

"We could go away," I whispered in his ear. "We could run out on Aarons and the Study Center and everyone, just go away somewhere."

He shook his head slowly. "Amy, don't."

"We could! I'll see Dr. Custer, and he'll tell me he can help, I *know* he will. I won't *need* the Study Center any more, or any other place, or anybody but you."

He didn't answer, and I knew there wasn't anything he could answer. Not then.

*

Friday, 26 May. Yesterday we went to Boston to see Dr. Custer, and now it looks as if it's all over. Now even I can't pretend that there's anything more to be done.

Next week Aarons will come down, and I'll go to work with him just the way he has it planned. He thinks we have three years of work ahead of us before anything can be published, before he can really be sure we have brought a latent into full use of his psi potential. Maybe so, I don't know. Maybe in three years I'll find some way to make myself care one way or the other. But I'll do it, anyway, because there's nothing else to do.

18

There was no anatomical defect—Dr. Custer was right about that. The eyes are perfect, beautiful gray eyes, he says, and the optic nerves and auditory nerves are perfectly functional. The defect isn't there. It's deeper. Too deep ever to change it.

What you no longer use, you lose, was what he said, apologizing because he couldn't explain it any better. It's like a price tag, perhaps. Long ago, before I knew anything at all, the psi was so strong it started compensating, bringing in more and more from *other* minds—such a wealth of rich, clear, interpreted visual and auditory impressions that there was never any need for my own. And because of that, certain hookups never got hooked up. That's only a theory, of course, but there isn't any other way to explain it.

But am I wrong to hate it? More than anything else in the world I want to *see* Lambertson, *see* him smile and light his pipe, *hear* him laugh. I want to know what color *really* is, what music *really* sounds like unfiltered through somebody else's ears.

I want to see a sunset, just once. Just once I want to see that mother duck take her ducklings down to the water. But I never will. Instead, I see and hear things nobody else can, and the fact that I am stone blind and stone deaf shouldn't make any difference. After all, I've always been that way.

Maybe next week I'll ask Aarons what he thinks about it. It should be interesting to hear what he says.